Sweet Dreams!
Sandy Wilber

GOODNIGHT MY HONEY BUNNIES

Story, concept, pictures adapted
from the original murals;
music and lyrics by Sandy Wilbur

Paintings by Kimberley A Ray

www.sandywilburmusic.com
info@sandywilburmusic.com
252 7th Avenue, Suite 17G
New York, NY 10001
212.217.2566

ISBN: 978-0-9907664-3-8

For free album download with book purchase,
please email: info@sandywilburmusic.com
Put FREE DOWNLOAD as subject,
and link will be emailed to you.

This book is dedicated with
lots of Love and Lullabies to:
James and Ronan ~ Sandy Wilbur
Lyric, Luca, and Livi ~ Kimberley A Ray

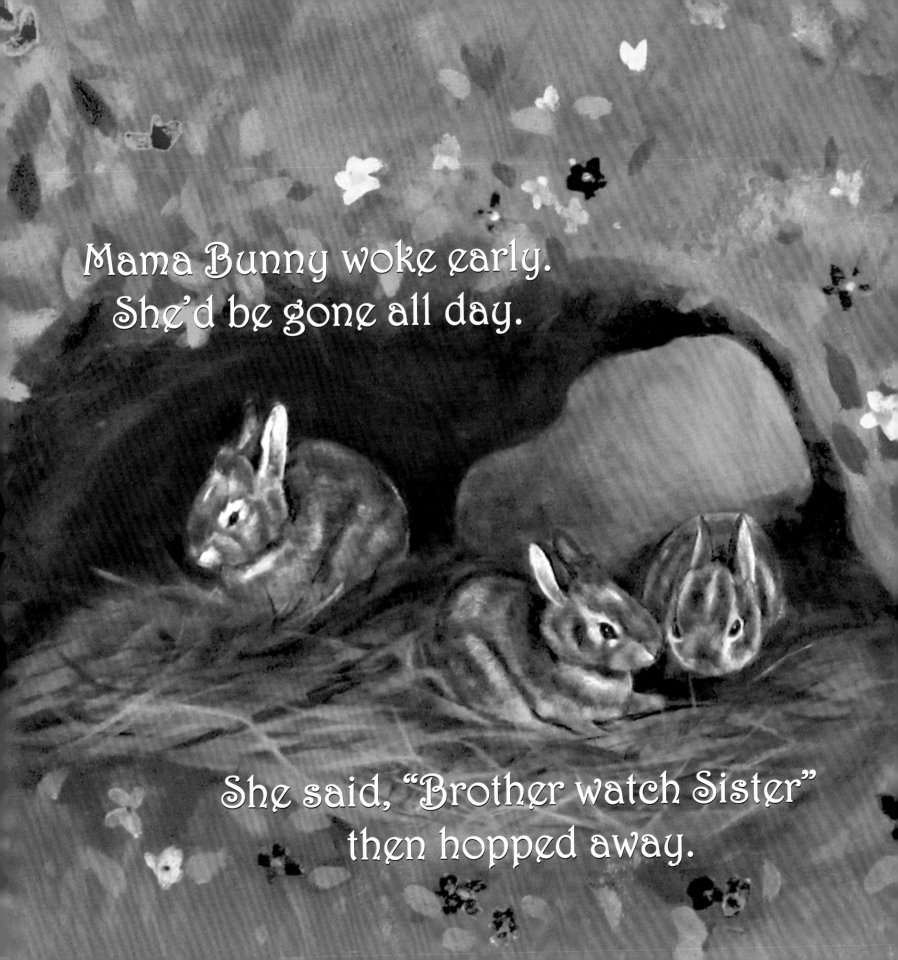

Mama Bunny woke early.
She'd be gone all day.

She said, "Brother watch Sister"
then hopped away.

They both peeked outside.
It was hard to ignore

the bright sunny field.

He said, "Time to explore!"

The flowers were beckoning,

beyond were some trees.

While a turtle walked by just as slow

as

you

please.

A butterfly flew
near a frog
on a log.
So they
followed that frog
to the edge
of a bog.

Just beyond was a pond.
The frog jumped right in.
"The water is warm,"
he said with a grin.

A dragonfly hovered,
but nothing seemed grander

than a fairy fishing
for a salamander!

They played by the pond
where the water lilies grow,
having such a good time...
Then what do you know?

The birds had stopped singing.
The sky had grown dim.

It was time to head home.
But where to begin...

The flowers looked different.

The
path
was
not
clear.

They were suddenly lost
and wished Mama was near.

"Have you seen our Mama?"
The ant shook his head.
"We certainly haven't,"
the porcupine said.

"Have you seen
our Mama?"

The owl said
"Who?"

So they
kept on going,
hoping
somebody
knew.

"Have you seen our Mama?" But the frog kept swaying to the beautiful music the fairy was playing.

"Have you seen our Mama?"
they asked a fairy
Who
was
rocking her baby.

"It's getting
quite scary!"

"I did see your Mama,
who was heading back home
just past that field.

You should NOT be alone!"

A full moon shone
as they found their way
back to their Mama.
What a V E R Y L O N G day!

Mama hugged them and kissed them.
She'd been worried, too.
It was way past their bedtime,
but she knew what to do.

She snuggled
them up,
and started
to sing
their favorite
songs
before tucking
them in.

Goodnight my Honey Bunnies.
Close your eyes and sleep tight.

May your favorite lullabies
bring sweet dreams tonight.

The End

GOODNIGHT MY HONEY BUNNIES

SANDY WILBUR

Produced, composed or arranged, and played by Sandy Wilbur
Sung by Diane Green
with additional guitar and other tracks by Nick DiFabbio
Mixed and mastered by Nick DiFabbio

1. HUSH LITTLE BABY
Arranged with Original Music
by Sandy Wilbur

Hush Little Baby, don't say a word,
Mama's gonna buy you a mockingbird.
And if that mockingbird don't sing,
Mama's gonna buy you a diamond ring.

And if that diamond ring turns to brass,
Mama's gonna buy you a looking glass.
And if that looking glass gets broke,
Mama's gonna buy you a billy goat.

And if that billy goat won't pull,
Mama's gonna buy you a cart and bull.
And if that cart and bull turn over,
Mama's gonna buy you a dog named Rover.

And if that dog named Rover don't bark,
Mama's gonna buy you a horse and cart.
And if that horse and cart fall down,
You'll still be the sweetest little baby in town.

2. THE SLUMBER BOAT
Arranged by Sandy Wilbur

Baby's boat's a silver moon, sailing in the sky,
Sailing o'er the sea of sleep, while the clouds float by.
Sail, Baby, Sail, out upon the sea,
Only don't forget to sail back again to me.

Baby's fishing for a dream, fishing near and far,
His line a silver moonbeam is, his tail a silver star.
Sail, Baby, Sail, out upon the sea,
Only don't forget to sail back again to me.

3. LA LA LULLABY
Composed and Arranged by Sandy Wilbur

La La La La Lullaby
All the stars are twinkling
La La La La Lullaby
The wind is softly singing
La La La La Lullaby

La La La La…

La La La La Lullaby
Trees are gently swaying
La La La La Lullaby
While the moon keeps saying
La La La La Lullaby

La La La La…

La La La La Lullaby
All the world is dreaming
La La La La Lullaby
Baby is a-sleeping
La La La La Lullaby

4. KUM-BA-YA
Arranged by Sandy Wilbur

Kum-ba-ya, my Lord, Kum-ba-ya.
Kum-ba-ya, my Lord, Kum-ba-ya.
Kum-ba-ya, my Lord, Kum-ba-ya.
Oh, Lord, Kum-ba-ya.

Someone's singing, Lord, Kum-ba-ya…
Someone's sleeping, Lord, Kum-ba-ya…

5. ALL THE PRETTY LITTLE HORSES
Arranged by Sandy Wilbur

Hush-A-Bye, don't you cry,
Go to sleep-y little baby.
When you wake you shall have
All the pretty little horses.
Bucks and bays

Dapples and grays,
All the pretty little horses.
Hush-A-Bye, don't you cry,
Go to sleep little baby.

6. COTTON CANDY TOWN
Lyrics, Music and Arrangement by Sandy Wilbur

Rainbow skies of gumdrops,
Lemon flavored buttercups,
All the trees are lollipops,
In Cotton Candy Town.

Rooftops made of chocolate bars,
Jelly beans for the moon and stars,
Peanut shells are used as cars
In Cotton Candy Town.

Everything you see is oh, so sweet,
And everything's to eat.

When you're tired you go to bed
In your house of gingerbread.
A marshmallow pillow for your head
In Cotton Candy Town.

7. SLEEP MY BABY SLEEP
Lyrics by Virginia Green
Composed and Arranged by Sandy Wilbur

Sleep, My Baby, Sleep
The moon has dimmed it's silv'ry light
The stars are twinkling in the night
While Mother holds you safe and tight
Sleep, My Baby, Sleep

Sleep, My Baby, Sleep
The birds are snuggled in their nest
And all the world's all peace and rest
You're cradled on your Mother's breast
Sleep, My Baby, Sleep

8. THE EVENING IS COMING
Arranged and Original Material Added by Sandy Wilbur

The Evening Is Coming, the sun sinks to rest,
The birds are all flying straight home to their nests.
"Caw, caw" says the crow as he flies overhead,
It's time little children were going to bed.

Here comes the pony, his work is all done,
Down through the meadow he takes a good run.
Up goes his heels, and down goes his head;
It's time little children were going to bed.

The Evening Is Coming, it's time now for bed;
The Evening Is Coming, put down your sweet head.

The Evening Is Coming, the sun sinks to rest;
The birds are all flying straight home to their nests.
"Caw, caw" says the crow as he flies overhead.
It's time little children were going to bed.

9. GOODNIGHT SONG
Composed and Arranged by Sandy Wilbur

Goodnight shoes and goodnight room
Morning will be coming soon
Goodnight dolls and goodnight ball
Goodnight picture on the wall

Goodnight mom and goodnight dad
Goodnight every dog and cat
Goodnight bed and goodnight light
Goodnight baby and sleep tight

10. BY'M BYE
Traditional with Additional Music Composed and Arranged by Sandy Wilbur

By'm Bye, By'm Bye
Stars shining number
Number one, number two, number three
Good Lord, By'm Bye, By'm Bye
Good Lord, By'm Bye

By'm Bye, By'm Bye
Stars shining number
Number four, number five, number six
Good Lord, By'm By'm Bye
Good Lord, By'm Bye

11. TWINKLE, TWINKLE LITTLE STAR
Arranged by Sandy Wilbur

Twinkle, Twinkle Little Star
How I wonder what you are.
Way up in the sky so bright,
Like a diamond in the night,
Twinkle, Twinkle Little Star,
How I wonder what you are.

12. RAISINS AND ALMONDS
Traditional Yiddish Song by Abraham Goldfaden Arranged by Sandy Wilbur

'Neath the cradle of my young son
Stands a goat, yes, a pure white one.
The little goat has been fated to wander;
That will be your fate, too.
Raisins sweet and almonds
Sleep, my little one sleep,
Sleep, my little one sleep.

13. ROCK-A-BYE BABY
Arranged by Sandy Wilbur

Rock-A-Bye Baby, on the treetop,
When the wind blows, the cradle will rock.
When the bough breaks, the cradle will fall
And down will come baby, cradle and all.

14. BRAHMS' LULLABY
Arranged by Sandy Wilbur

Lullaby, and good night
With roses bedight
With lilies be spread
In Baby's wee bed
Lay thee down now and rest
May thy slumber be blessed
Lay thee down now and rest
May thee slumber be blessed

15. THANK YOU
Composed and Arranged by Sandy Wilbur

Thank you, God, for lullabies
And for the birds that sing.
Thank you for the flowers that bloom
And for the dreams I dream.

Thank you for the ones I love
And all the things they do.
Thank you, God, for being there
To watch me all night through.

Thank you for tonight.
The moon is shining bright,
The sandman will be on his way,
Tomorrow is another day.

Thank you for the little things
I sometimes fail to see.
Thank you for the day I've had
And Thank You, God, for me.

16. ALL THROUGH THE NIGHT
Arranged by Sandy Wilbur

Sleep, my child and peace attend thee
All Through The Night.
Guardian Angels God will wend thee
All Through The Night.

Soft the drowsy hours are creeping,
Hill and vale in slumber sleeping,
I my loving vigil keeping
All Through The Night, All Through The Night,
All Through The Night.

ABOUT THE AUTHOR

In addition to creating the concept and story for "Goodnight My Honey Bunnies," Sandy Wilbur is a forensic musicologist and award-winning composer / lyricist with over forty songs recorded and five chart singles to her credit. Sandy is also the creator / composer / producer of the series "Learning History Through Music" for grades K–8. The recently released book of the same title includes eight educational videos, three CDs, lesson plans, sheet music and historical chapters. She and her husband split their time between their Vermont farm and New York City. More information can be found at *www.sandywilburmusic.com*.

ABOUT THE PAINTER

Kimberley Ray's love for art, nature and animals has led her to become a renowned mural painter. Her murals grace private homes and businesses throughout the United States and beyond. Kim lives on a peaceful stone cottage farm in Vermont with her beloved husband, a menagerie of animals including two bunnies named Flower and Peter Piper. These animals are the inspirational models for many of her paintings and book illustrations. More information can be found at *www.kimraymurals.com*.